Discover the DARK

Firespell
LOUISE COOPER

The Lost Brides
THERESA RADCLIFFE

DARK
ENCHANTMENT

The Hounds of Winter
LOUISE COOPER

DARK
ENCHANTMENT

House of Thorns
JUDY DELAGHTY

DARK
ENCHANTMENT

Valley of Wolves
THERESA RADCLIFFE

DARK
ENCHANTMENT

Blood Dance
LOUISE COOPER

Other titles in the DARK ENCHANTMENT series

Kiss of the Vampire

J. B. CALCHMAN

PUFFIN BOOKS

For Carla and Andrew

PUFFIN BOOKS

Published by the Penguin Group
Penguin Books Ltd, 27 Wrights Lane, London W8 5TZ, England
Penguin Books USA Inc., 375 Hudson Street, New York,
New York 10014, USA
Penguin Books Australia Ltd, Ringwood, Victoria, Australia
Penguin Books Canada Ltd, 10 Alcorn Avenue, Toronto, Ontario,
Canada M4V 3B2
Penguin Books (NZ) Ltd, 182–190 Wairau Road, Auckland 10,
New Zealand

Penguin Books Ltd, Registered Offices: Harmondsworth, Middlesex,
England

First published 1996
1 3 5 7 9 10 8 6 4 2

Filmset by Datix International Limited, Bungay, Suffolk
Printed in England by Clays Ltd, St Ives plc
Set in 12/14pt Monophoto Sabon

THE FUNERAL

OAKPORT, MAINE

THE CHURCHYARD was perched on the top of a cliff. A line of black spruce trees was all that prevented it from slipping into the ocean. Down below, the water swirled and a mist rose, like steam, seeping into the crags of the dark rock as it made its ascent.

Three fresh gravestones had been set into the earth that morning, and now, in the last of the light, four figures approached them. The preacher led the way, his robes skimming the damp ground as he took his position. The others followed: a woman whose ill-assorted clothes might have come from a dressing-up box; a tall man whose thick, blond hair was like a flame against his dark coat; and last, a child, a boy, struggling to keep up, tumbling forward towards the graves.

There was another person in that churchyard, hidden among the spruces at the cliff-edge. His eyes strained to watch the funeral procession. The preacher had begun to speak, but there was no hope of hearing him from this distance. The old man's crumpled mouth opened and closed, fish-like, his words seemingly making no dent in the air. The others huddled together, as if gaining strength from each other. The watcher had an overwhelming desire to turn and run, but he knew that it was out of the question. Whatever he felt, the child was more important.

A sudden shot of pain bore through him and he lurched back, falling on to the bed of pine needles. It was the same sensation as before – as if his veins were overloaded with blood. He froze, numb, as the pain took hold. His eyes locked on the circling branches above. He let the scent of the pines wash into him. Gradually, the tenseness subsided and the pain crept away.

Relieved, he clawed back up to his feet, his hand brushing the bandage on his neck. As he steadied himself, he drew his hand away and saw that the tips of his fingers were scarlet.

When his eyes returned to the funeral party, he saw the preacher beckon the man to the graves. In response, the man stooped to the ground and grabbed a handful of earth from the mound beside the first grave. He stepped to the edge of the hole and released the earth. The watcher imagined the echo as it thudded against the coffin below.

The man repeated his actions at the next grave. The rain had started again but, unflinching, the preacher, woman and child stood and watched. The man moved on to the third grave.

This time as he threw the earth, it would not move from his hand. He tried again, but still it would not shift. He turned and the watcher could see the look of horror on his face.

The woman rushed forward, leaving the boy's side. She seized the man by the wrist and tugged at the earth. Suddenly, it came away, leaving a dark stain. The woman twisted the man's palm up towards the sky and, as the rain fell, scrubbed away as if she were washing a child's fingers.

The boy stood alone in the centre of the churchyard, trembling. Instinctively, the watcher moved to the edge of the trees. Could this be the chance he had been waiting for? He quickly calculated the distance between them. He could do it. It would all be over then. The circle would be complete.

But if he failed? If he was seen? The others might be scared, but that wouldn't stop them. It would all begin again. And the child would be lost to him for ever. He recoiled, with a pain far worse than that from the blood-wound. He could not do this. Not yet. He would have to make new plans.

The preacher was leading them back into the church. The woman turned and took the child's left hand. The man followed behind. As the rain grew heavier, they started to run. Once again, the boy struggled to keep pace. As the heavy church door slammed shut behind them, a bolt of lightning sliced through the sky. Thunder followed.

Alone in the churchyard, the watcher stepped out from his hiding-place. Lumps of earth clung to his boots. He realized how foolish he had been to think he could have captured the boy. He could move only slowly now, as once he had through the ocean, the undertow tugging at his legs. The thunder and lightning crashed around him as he stood before the three graves. The others' footprints had already been washed away.

He watched the water worming its way into the newly carved marble and shuddered as he read the inscriptions.

Adam Culler, 1952–1995. Beloved husband of Charlotte and father of Alexander and Charles . . .

Charlotte Baines Culler, 1954–1995 . . .

Alexander Culler, 1978–1995. Son of Adam and Charlotte. 'In their death they were not divided' . . .

The tears that had begun to form froze with the shock of reading his own name. His finger traced the carved letters on the icy marble. *Alexander Culler*. He still could not believe what had happened.

As another flash of lightning struck, the pain

within him seemed to respond, pushing through his veins and towards the wound. And the warm river of blood gushed from his neck to his shoulder and down to join the sea of mud below.

CHAPTER I

ST DOVE'S, CORNWALL
SEVERAL WEEKS LATER

'YOU DON'T KNOW anything about him.'
'And if I don't ask, I never will!'
'You can't.'
'I can.'
'He could be dangerous.'
'Don't be daft.'
'Remember what happened to Juliet.'
'Yes, but . . .'
'But you don't believe in . . .'

The argument, if it could be called that, was interrupted by the door opening. Just another couple of tourists coming into the Green Room to get a coffee and something to eat after a stroll along the beach. As Greeny settled them with a menu and began to chit-chat, Ella remained by the window, watching the boy outside.

For the past week, they had argued about him. Ella was curious to know his story, but Greeny believed he was best left alone. Of course, her aunt had strong views about boys and men, after the latest upheavals in her own personal life. But Ella wasn't just being awkward or stubborn. There was something about the boy which drew her to watch him, even though he never appeared to notice her.

The steam from the coffee machine had clouded up the window and Ella wiped her hand over the pane to make a peep-hole. He was standing in the usual place, his eyes locked on the ocean. There were plenty of people who came down to look at the sea, but this was different. He seemed mesmerized by the waves.

It was a blustery morning and the wind twisted the long dark strands of his hair. Otherwise, he was as still as a statue, his hands buried deep in the pockets of his coat. His clothes were another mystery. In spite of the breeze, it was a warm summer's day. Everyone else was wandering around in T-shirts and shorts, but he wore a thick winter coat and heavy black boots. Both were scuffed with dirt much darker than the sand.

'Ella.'

Ella turned and could tell from Greeny's expression that she had been trying to attract her attention for a while. She followed the line of Greeny's gaze and went over to pick up the two coffee cups and take them over to the couple. She placed them on the table, smiling vacantly, and returned to the window. It had steamed up again and again she made herself a porthole.

It was infuriating the way his hair flapped

around his face, preventing her from gaining a proper view of it. She knew from other times how handsome he was. Perhaps it was the unnatural stillness, but he seemed to her like a sculpture, his features soft and smooth as aged stone.

'Excuse me. Excuse me, miss . . .'

Ella turned, unable to blot out the anger from her expression. Why couldn't they leave her alone?

'We're ready to order now. Can you tell your mother, we'd like . . .'

Deciding it wasn't worth correcting them, Ella noted their requests and relayed them to Greeny, who was washing pots in the kitchen. She didn't stay long, anxious to resume her look-out. As she regained her position at the window, she saw with sadness that the boy had gone. She looked down the beach and noticed that the tide had turned. He always left just as the tide started to come in.

The door to the café swung open and three boys ambled inside. They had been surfing and were still wearing their wet suits, rolled down to their waists, along with bright T-shirts and 'bajas' – thick, brightly striped, hooded shirts.

'How was the surf?' the male tourist inquired, looking up from his soup.

'Spectacular,' one of the boys answered, running his hands through his curly blond hair and making his way over to Ella. 'Hello, stranger,' he said, taking her in his arms and nuzzling her neck.

'Ooh, that explains it!' giggled the woman. 'She's been staring out of that window like a zombie. I thought something was wrong, but she was obviously watching you!'

Everyone laughed but Ella.

'Did you see me out there? What did you think?'

Ella unwrapped his arms from her waist. 'You were great, Teddy. I'll go get some Cokes.'

'So, have you heard about the Vampire of St Dove's?' Ella heard Teddy ask the couple, as she opened up the refrigerator.

'I was reading about that in our guidebook,' the man replied. 'It was during plague times, wasn't it? He roamed the streets of the town, drinking the blood of the dying.'

His wife tutted. She clearly didn't think this was a suitable mealtime conversation.

'Oh yes, everyone knows about that old vampire,' breezed Teddy. 'I'm talking about the new vampire!'

The man looked up in curiosity. Greeny shot a warning look at Teddy, but he was on a roll.

'Oh yes, indeed! It happened a little over a week ago. A girl walking home late at night . . . you get the picture? Next morning, she was found by the side of the road, with two little puncture marks in her neck.'

The man gasped and the woman went pale.

'She was alive,' Greeny interrupted.

'Barely,' Teddy retorted, 'and she hasn't spoken since.'

Ella was about to pass Teddy a Coke when he wandered over to the table and rested a hand on the woman's shoulder. 'Want to know the best bit? The girl was a waitress here.'

The woman turned a shade of green, pushed back her chair and rushed out into the air. The man followed, frowning. Greeny ran to the door and looked on helplessly as the couple headed away along the beach.

'Teddy Stone, you're bad for business,' Greeny said, closing the door.

Teddy laughed and drained his Coke. 'Please, Mrs Green, can Ella come out to play?' he said, affecting a child's voice.

Greeny began to smile. 'Off you go, then,' she said.

The boys ambled back out on to the beach, where the sun was shining brightly. Ella followed, her hand in Teddy's.

'You have a good time,' laughed Greeny, going off to clear the debris of the tourist couple's lunch.

Ella said nothing. She couldn't get him out of her head – the mysterious boy who came each day to watch the sea.

CHAPTER II

ELLA LAY BACK on the rug, her dark sun-glasses filtering the strong afternoon sun-light, and tossed the paperback to one side. She must have read the same sentence a hundred times. She couldn't concentrate at all. The heat seemed to have sapped all her energy.

She reached into her bag and fumbled for her Walkman. It was already loaded with a tape she'd put together of all her favourite songs. She slipped in the ear plugs, closed her eyes and turned up the volume, luxuriating in the familiar music.

She hadn't been listening for long when she became aware of a shadow over her, blocking the sun. She opened her eyes and removed the earphones.

'Ashley. How was the water?'

'Perfect!' Ashley Stone beamed, patting herself dry. 'I just love the water. Not quite like the boys, of course. They're obsessed! But it's so refreshing. Oh, Ella . . . I'm sorry. I forgot you can't swim.'

'That's all right.'

'I never imagined Teddy would go out with someone who didn't like the water,' Ashley said, combing her hair. 'Of course, he'd love to teach you.'

Ella had no desire for Teddy to teach her to swim. Still, there was no point in arguing with Ashley. She would soon latch on to a new topic of conversation.

'Scott's going to teach *me* how to surf,' Ashley continued, opening a tube of sun cream and massaging it over her shoulders. 'Now, that should be fun! I mean, Daddy tried to teach me when Teddy and I were both little. And Teddy's even given me one or two lessons. But there's more of an incentive for Scott to show me . . . if you know what I mean!'

Realizing that there was going to be no end to Ashley's chatter, Ella decided to make herself comfortable and rolled over, sprawling on the rug.

'Shall I do your back?' Ashley inquired.

Ella nodded. Ashley squirted a cold blob of sun screen on to her warm shoulders.

'You've become so quiet lately, Ella,' gabbled Ashley, drawing the cream down Ella's shoulder-blades. 'Is it this vampire business? You know, I'm sure there's a logical explanation. I mean, I know all about the stories of St Dove's during the plague, but I'm sure that's all they were . . . stories. And now! Don't get me wrong, I'm scared too. I mean perhaps there is some maniac on the loose. Unless –'

'Let's not talk about it,' Ella said. 'Why don't

you tell me what you're going to wear to the party at Smugglers' Cove?'

'The grand opening of the Cave, you mean? Well, let me see . . .'

Ella had struck gold. There was nothing Ashley enjoyed discussing more than clothes. As she rambled on, weighing up the pros and cons of one outfit against another, Ella closed her eyes and let the words drift over her.

She was brought to attention by a shower of icy drops on her body. She twisted round as Teddy leaned over her. He had just come out of the sea and was dripping wet. She was about to protest but he silenced her with a kiss. Over his shoulder, she saw Ashley rubbing cream into Scott's shoulders. Things were getting pretty serious between the two of them.

Jeff, meanwhile, was encountering some difficulty, rubbing sun cream into the well of his back. He had broken up with his latest girlfriend, Laura, the previous week and was taking it hard. Feeling sorry for him, Ella offered to help. He ran over gratefully and crouched down in front of her, eager to chat. Sighing, Teddy sauntered off to fetch a drink from the cool box.

'So, what's going on tonight?' Scott asked Teddy as he passed.

'I thought we might drive down the coast. Apparently, there's this great new place on the Lizard. There's a barbecue and a live band tonight.'

There were nods and sounds of enthusiasm from everyone but Ella. 'I have to work tonight,' she said and then, in response to Teddy's groans, 'you knew that.'

Of course he acted dumb, making it seem as though she was spoiling everyone's fun.

'Look, you can go without me,' Ella said, grabbing a Coke.

'I didn't start going out with you so that I could spend my evenings alone,' Teddy snapped. As if on cue, the others turned away and began their own conversations.

'Look, Teddy,' Ella said calmly, 'things are hard for Greeny right now. We don't know how long Juliet will be away and, in case you hadn't noticed, the café is busier than ever. People come from miles around to see where "the vampire" claimed his first victim. It's morbid but it is good for business. Just try to be patient, Teddy.'

'Yeah, I suppose,' he said, looking deep into her eyes, 'it's just difficult to be patient where you're concerned. You know I want to be with you all the time.'

'Except when you're surfing,' Ella said, trying to lighten the mood.

'Don't joke,' Teddy replied. 'I've never felt this way about anyone before.' He drew her face up towards his and they kissed.

'Why don't you guys head out to that place at the Lizard tonight and if I can get away later, I will,' Ella offered.

The others agreed and decided it was time they were heading home to get ready. They packed up their stuff and headed up the cliff path to where Scott's red MG and Teddy's black VW convertible were parked.

In a moment, the stereos were clicked into action, the shades were in place and the two cars were racing back to the other side of town. With some of Teddy's favourite rock music blaring from the stereo, it was too noisy to speak and Ella lost herself in her own thoughts. Before she knew it, Teddy was bringing the VW to a halt at the back of the Green Room.

'Wow, is that a Harley?' he said, flipping up his sun-glasses and ogling the motor bike, propped to one side of the café door.

Teddy jumped out of his seat and went over to have a closer look. The bike was somewhat battered and rusted, but it retained its classic style. 'This baby hasn't seen the light of day for a while,' he decided. 'I wonder who it belongs to.'

'Who cares?' snorted Ashley, from the back of the car. 'You'd never catch me riding on that heap of junk. It looks like it's going to fall to pieces any moment.'

'You just don't understand, sis,' Teddy said, smiling. He turned to Ella. 'I'll phone you when I get in with the details of this place. You'll see if you can come along later?'

She nodded and kissed him goodbye. He

climbed back into the car and started it up, honking the horn loudly as he drove away. Ella pushed open the door to the café and stepped inside, her eyes taking a moment to grow accustomed to the darkness. The café was empty, but Ella knew from experience that it wouldn't be for much longer. In an hour the place would be full of kids from all over town. She was about to step into the kitchen when Greeny came out of it. Seeing Ella, she smiled broadly.

'Did you have a nice afternoon?'

Ella nodded. 'I know I'm a bit late. I'll just go up to the flat and grab a shower and I'll be ready to help.'

'It's OK, love,' Greeny said, 'I've got some good news. I've hired someone new! And, better yet, they can start tonight.'

'Oh, that's great!' Ella said. 'Who is she?'

'Come and see,' Greeny said, pushing open the kitchen door.

Ella followed her inside and was amused to see that Greeny's new helper was already elbows deep in washing-up — a shock of dark hair bowed over the sink.

'Alex,' Greeny said, 'I'd like you to meet my niece. Ella, this is Alex Culler.'

Ella smiled as Alex turned. Then her heart missed a beat. It wasn't a girl at all but a boy; the boy she had been watching each day. She had imagined their meeting a hundred times, but not here, not like this. She didn't know what to say. Just looking at him made her uneasy.

'I'll go and . . . change the coffee filters,' Greeny said, winking at Ella before the kitchen door swung shut behind her.

Ella felt trapped. This was what she had wanted – a chance to be alone with him, to ask him who he was and where he had come from and why he watched the sea as if his life depended upon it? And yet, she couldn't bring herself to speak, let alone ask such probing questions.

'She told me, you know.'

'What?'

Ella couldn't decide whether she was more surprised because he had struck up a conversation, or because he had an American accent.

'Greeny. She told me what happened to Juliet.'

Ella was silent. If only she could think of something, *anything*, to say.

'I'm sorry,' he said. 'Would you rather not talk about it?'

'No! No, it's OK.'

Now he seemed unable to find the right words.

'Do you . . .' she began, 'do you believe in . . .'

Catching his eye, she was unable to finish the sentence. He was looking at her with such an intensity, as if he was staring deep into her, through her.

'Do I believe?' He repeated the question to himself and paused before answering. 'I guess I don't know what I believe any more.'

She waited for him to continue, to explain what he meant. But he turned away and busied himself with the things in the sink. Ella had the feeling that once again she was watching him from the other side of the window and he was completely unaware of her existence.

Later That Night . . .

I HAVE SENSED the hunger building all day and, as night falls, I know what is going to happen. When the town is dark and almost deserted, I make my way to the cliff edge. There's a place I've found there where I can sit and listen to the waves. The sound scares me, yet it draws me to it.

I lose track of the time I spend there, lulled by the noise of the sea and the patterns of the shifting darkness, broken only by the flashes from the lighthouse. At times like this, I can't help but think of the journey I have made. Such a long way. When I think of who I was, of where I've come from, I marvel at the strange paths my life has taken.

Life. It's hard to believe that this *is* life and not death. And yet, there have been better times. Perhaps there can be again.

The hunger is building. It's like this every time. It starts small, like an itch, a dull ache, inside me. Gradually, it becomes more acute. Finally, it tears through me, pulsating with a life of its own. Then, I have only one need and there is only one way of satisfying it.

I see beyond the cliff-top trees. I see deep

down into the sea. I see to the end of this road. And I see the girl, walking towards me through the shadows. I see the girl and I know that my hunger will soon be satisfied.

I decide to wait, to let her come to me. The trees will give us shelter, away from the road. I *can* wait. Now that I know she is coming.

She draws level with me and I reach out, taking her hand. She turns. For an instant we stand face to face. We are mirror images of each other – the same height, the same long dark hair. I smile. I want to win her trust.

It is over quickly for her. Time runs differently for me. I am over-anxious and her silky hair slips through my fingers when I try to lift it away from her neck. I try again and, this time, succeed. I have no need to restrain her now. She is perfectly still. It is as if she knows everything.

My lips brush her neck and I can feel the flow of blood beneath the skin. I bite. She jerks at the impact but does not move again. Quickly, I draw the blood up towards my lips. I drink thirstily.

I know when to stop. I step back and see that she has closed her eyes. The breeze lifts the threads of hair from her neck and I watch this, entranced, for a time.

Then I lay her down where I know they will find her.

CHAPTER III

'**I CAN'T BELIEVE** you hired him,' Ella said as she and Greeny sat down to breakfast the following morning.

'No, but you're glad I did, aren't you?' her aunt replied, sipping coffee from her favourite pottery mug.

Ella blushed. 'Yesterday, you were telling me how dangerous he was. What made you change your mind?'

'Yes, that was wrong of me. I shouldn't have judged him on his appearance. I really ought to know better than that by now. He came in here and asked about the vacancy – he'd seen the card in the window – and he was just very sweet.'

Ella smiled, thinking back to the previous evening. In the time she had spent with Alex, they had scarcely spoken. He had told her next to nothing about himself. And yet, she felt more strongly than ever that there was something special about him, something which connected the two of them.

'You like him!' Greeny said, pouring another mug of coffee and offering Ella a freshly baked muffin.

'What's not to like?' Ella said, blushing.

'And where does this leave Mr Stone?' her aunt inquired.

Ella shrugged. 'When I started going out with Teddy, it was like the most magical thing, a fairy-tale. I mean, everyone wants to be with him, but *he* chose *me*. And he is very handsome and everything . . .'

'But . . .' persisted Greeny.

'But I'm not exactly sure why we're together any more.'

Ella and Teddy had been going out with each other for almost a year. Lately, however, the spark seemed to have died. They still had fun, but the old excitement wasn't there. Perhaps that was what intrigued her about Alex. Getting to know him would be like starting to unravel a complex mystery; whereas she could predict pretty well all of Teddy's thoughts and actions and moods.

'Well, just be careful,' was Greeny's advice. 'Teddy Stone won't take rejection easily and we still don't know very much about Alex.'

'You're not going to tell me again that he's dangerous, are you?'

'No, but he is hurting. I can feel it. And he's run away from something, something bad. You'd better tread carefully, for his sake . . . and your own.'

Greeny buried herself in her newspaper and Ella looked out through the window to the beach. The sun had already cast a pool of gold over the sand. It had all the makings of a perfect day.

They cleared up the breakfast things and were just setting out the menus when Alex drew up outside on his bike. He came inside, unstrapping his helmet.

'You're bright and early,' Greeny said. 'Coffee?'

'No thanks,' Alex said, walking past them into the kitchen. He didn't even say hello to Ella. She felt her spirits sink.

Greeny placed a comforting hand on Ella's shoulder. 'Rome wasn't built in a day, love,' she whispered.

They burst into giggles. The giggles grew into laughter until Ella could feel her sides aching.

'What are you two laughing about?' Teddy asked, closing the door of the café behind him. He kissed Ella and grabbed a chair. Greeny said she'd get him some coffee and disappeared, still chuckling, into the kitchen.

'Where did you get to last night?' Teddy inquired after Greeny had gone.

'I'm sorry,' Ella said, feeling the hysteria subside. 'I couldn't get away. We had a really busy night. Did you have a good time?'

'Without you?' Teddy shrugged. 'Impossible! I see the Harley's still outside . . .'

Greeny reappeared from the kitchen with a mug of coffee for Teddy. She beckoned Alex to follow her.

'Teddy,' Greeny said, 'I'd like you to meet Alex Culler. He's going to be helping out around here. Alex, this is ... one of our regulars, Teddy Stone.'

The boys shook hands. Ella suddenly felt awkward. Until yesterday, Alex had been her secret. And secrets were few and far between in a town as small as St Dove's. Now that Alex was working at the café, everything was going to change.

'Culler,' Teddy said. 'You're related to the old guy who repairs clocks in the high street?'

Alex nodded but said nothing. Ella smiled. Why should Teddy be any more successful than her in getting Alex to talk about himself?

'Is that your Harley outside?' Teddy persisted.

'Not exactly,' Alex said.

'It belongs to Gabriel Culler,' Greeny explained, seeing that Alex's reticence was starting to infuriate Teddy. 'It was rusting to pieces in his garage. Alex cleaned it up and it seems to be going OK.'

'Maybe I could borrow it sometime,' Teddy said.

'Maybe.'

'Here's an idea,' Teddy said. 'Have you heard of Smugglers' Cove? It's a theme park — the closest thing in England to Disneyworld. My family owns it and we're having a little party there on Saturday night to celebrate the opening of our new night-club. Why don't you come along, Alex? It'll be a good chance to get to know everyone. Ella will fill you in on all the details.'

'OK,' Alex said, retreating into the kitchen.

'Talkative guy!' Teddy exclaimed as the door swung shut after Alex. 'What's his story?'

'Maybe he doesn't have a story,' Ella said, doing her best to act uninterested.

'Everyone has a story! And I'd say Alex Culler has a very interesting story indeed. How do you suppose he's related to the old man – what's his name, Gabriel? – for a start?'

Before Ella could come up with an answer, the door burst open and a young boy, perhaps eight or nine years old, ran into the café. He was out of breath and his eyes were bulging. He tried to speak but he couldn't get the words out.

Greeny poured him a glass of water. 'Here, sit down, tell us what's wrong.'

The boy shook his head. Without speaking, he ran over and grabbed Teddy's arm, indicating for him to follow.

'Careful!' Teddy said. 'This shirt cost a fortune.'

He followed the boy out on to the beach. Ella and Greeny rushed to the door of the café. Alex came out to see what was going on and joined the others at the doorway, watching as Teddy ran after the boy up the cliff path. They disappeared for some minutes. When they reappeared, Teddy was carrying a girl's body slumped over his shoulders.

'It's Lucy Vale,' Teddy gasped. 'She's unconscious, maybe . . .'

'Oh my . . .' Greeny interrupted, 'I'll call an ambulance.'

Alex rushed over to help Teddy, while Ella tried to soothe the young boy. He was still in a state of shock.

'Here, put her down over here,' Greeny instructed, tapping the buttons on the phone. 'Yes, I need an ambulance . . . The Green Room Café . . . Now!'

She hung up and rushed over to join the others. Lucy's eyes were open and stared wildly at them. Her dress was torn and smudged with dirt. She was wearing only one shoe and her other foot was red and swollen. Her hair was bedraggled and her skin was deathly pale.

Teddy grabbed a cushion and made a pillow for her on the floor. As he set her head down, it rolled to one side. There, on the girl's neck, were two dark puncture marks. They were spaced perhaps three or four centimetres apart and purplish-black where the blood had collected and dried.

'They're the same marks!' Greeny cried. 'The exact same marks Juliet had.'

There was silence in the café until finally the little boy spoke. He gulped some water, set down the glass and shuddered.

'It's the vampire. He's come back.'

CHAPTER IV

'VAMPIRE OR NO vampire, I said the party goes ahead!' Richard Stone was not one to mince words, nor to let the small matter of a vampire on the loose interfere with the opening of the Cave. As Ella followed Teddy and his father to the night-club's entrance, she couldn't help thinking about Lucy Vale and Juliet Partridge. There would be no party for them tonight.

'Isn't this exciting?' Rowena Stone said, following behind Ella. Ella smiled back at Teddy's mother, nodding.

She passed through the entrance and caught sight of the passage ahead. A green light exposed the slimy walls. She was surprised that they hadn't tried to disguise the natural setting. As she drew nearer, she reached out her fingers to touch the slime. She laughed, realizing that it was a brilliant fake. She should have known.

Just then, a spray of mist enveloped her and Teddy drew her towards him. Unable to see more than a few paces in front of her, Ella walked on through the passage until the mist swirled away and she found herself at the top of a spiralling stairway, plummeting through the rock.

She followed Teddy on to the stairway, turning briefly to glimpse Rowena's and Ashley's excited faces as they too emerged from the mist. There was the sound of running water ahead. Ella looked down and saw that Teddy was about to be soaked by a waterfall.

'Wait!' she called, but he was already beneath the stream. Miraculously, the water avoided him, flowing into the rock on the other side. Ella walked beneath the spray and found that she too was untouched by the water.

She hurried on down the twisting stairway, catching up with Teddy and his father at the bottom. They were engulfed in another strand of mist.

'Impressed?' asked Richard Stone. As he spoke, he stepped to one side. The mist dissolved and Ella gasped. They were standing in a vast cavern. She had hardly had a chance to take it in, when dance music suddenly began to play and lights started to spin, high up in the roof.

'I've never seen anything like it, Dad!' Teddy said.

Rowena, Ashley and Scott had caught them up. The other guests were close behind. As people arrived in the cavern, there were gasps of appreciation, followed by laughter. The Stones had done it again.

'Let's dance!' Teddy cried, pulling Ella towards the centre of the dance-floor. Ashley and Scott followed.

As she began to move, Ella felt the pounding music pulse through her. The lights seemed to orbit around them, the multi-coloured beams reflected in Teddy's eyes. A strobe came on and Ella was shocked by how it transformed everyone. In the broken light, even Teddy and Ashley's smooth features seemed strange and sinister.

Richard and Rowena Stone joined them on the dance-floor, encouraging the other guests to follow. Ella glanced around, feeling dizzy from the noise and the lights and the endless flow of bodies. She was grateful when the music came to an end. Everyone started to cheer. She turned and saw that Richard Stone had a microphone in his hand. When the cheering subsided, he began to speak.

'Hi, everybody. Thanks for coming. This is a very special night for Smugglers' Cove and for the Stone family. They said we couldn't do it! Well, they were wrong. We *did* do it! Now, let's get the music back on and let's party!'

There were more cheers as the music and flashing lights came on again. Richard Stone rejoined his family.

'Well done, darling!' Rowena said, kissing her husband on the cheek.

'You know it almost didn't happen,' Richard Stone said, frowning.

'What do you mean, Daddy?' Ashley inquired.

'It's this vampire nonsense!' her father replied. 'I had a call from the police this morning. People are saying there should be a curfew in St Dove's. Just when we're ahead of Alton Towers. This is all we need. We're hardly into peak season.'

'You know Lucy Vale hasn't spoken since the attack?' Ashley informed him. 'Just like Juliet. It *is* kind of scary.'

Richard Stone cut her dead with a glance. 'I don't know what happened to those girls, but I do know this: there's no such thing as vampires.'

There was an awkward silence. Ella glanced away, her eyes sweeping across the sea of dancers. There, at the foot of the stairway, was Alex. His eyes met hers and they walked towards each other, meeting at the edge of the dance-floor.

'Hi,' Alex said.

'I'm glad you came,' Ella said. 'I didn't think you would.'

'I'm sorry.'

'What for?'

'If I've seemed rude to you, or your friends. I guess I'm still in shock . . .'

'It's OK,' Ella said. 'Really! I know how hard it is to settle in a new place. And believe me, St Dove's takes quite a bit of getting used to.'

'Have you lived here long?' Alex asked.

'Greeny and I only moved down last year.

From London.' Ella waited for him to ask another question but he didn't. 'So you see, Alex,' she continued, 'I've been there. I know what you're going through.'

He said nothing. His face seemed closed to her again.

'Come on.' She grabbed his arm. 'Let's get a drink.'

They stood at a corner of the bar, drinking Cokes in silence. Around them, there was a hum of chatter as the rest of St Dove's caught up on the gossip and exchanged views on the 'vampire' attacks.

'Do you really think there is a vampire in St Dove's?' Alex asked suddenly. The strength of his stare was unsettling.

'I don't know what I think,' Ella said carefully. 'I mean, we saw the marks on Lucy. What do *you* think?'

He shrugged. 'I think sometimes our eyes deceive us. We see one thing when in fact the truth is quite different.'

Was he trying to tell her something about himself, about his life? Ella tried to get her mind around the riddle but made no headway. She was about to ask him what he meant, when he spoke again.

'It's time I was going.'

'But you've only just arrived,' she protested. He was slipping away from her again, just when she had thought she was getting closer.

'I think your boy-friend wants you,' Alex said.

Ella glanced at Teddy out of the corner of her eye, signalling to her from the middle of the crowd. She turned to say goodbye to Alex but he had already gone. She looked over towards the stairs. Unable to stop herself, she moved through the crowd and started to climb the stairway.

She could hear the echo of his steps just ahead of her as she moved up through the falling water and swirling mist, back to the entrance. The bouncer quickly extinguished a cigarette and nervously dusted himself down.

'Hello, Miss Ryder. Having fun?'

Ella ignored him and carried on, into the darkness, her eyes ranging left and right. She could see no sign of Alex. Suddenly, she heard an engine roar into action. She turned, unable to pinpoint the direction of the sound. Then, out of the darkness, Alex's motor bike came flying towards her.

'Alex, wait!'

He seemed neither to hear nor see her. He drove on past. She ran after him but it was no use. He was already through the theme-park gates. Ella slowed to a standstill and caught her breath.

'Who are you, Alex Culler?' She heard the words fall from her mouth. 'Who are you and what are you doing in St Dove's?'

LATER THAT NIGHT . . .

THE PARTY IS over. The gates to the theme park are closed. And the party-goers get out of their cars and taxis into their beds. They must be tired from all that laughter, all that dancing. I too am tired.

There's a sliver of moonlight tonight, but it barely cuts through the clouds. It's the thinnest of light to find your way home by. It reminds me of something long past . . .

I can hear music. The plucking of strings. Somewhere near. Through the trees? I see! Here he sits, picking at the strings of a guitar. I stop and listen. So, he comes here too, to play his music. It is a perfect place, made more perfect by the darkness and the music. I feel . . . soothed. But I can also feel my hunger stirring. Tonight, it will be easy. Tonight, it will be him.

His fingers lift from the strings and he turns, the shadow of the trees keeping half his face in darkness. He sees me standing there, leaning against the branches.

I compliment him on his music and he smiles. He tells me that the others don't understand. That is why he has come to this place at this hour.

He isn't scared. I feel almost that he wants this. As I draw nearer and steady his neck, he remains still. Tonight, my touch is certain, precise.

I drink. He sits, perfectly still. The guitar is balanced on his lap, his fingers resting on the smooth wood surface. When I am done, I back away. A solitary drop of blood escapes from his neck and spills on to the wood.

I take a handkerchief and wipe it up. Then, I walk away. Behind me, I still seem to hear the music, even though his fingers are still.

CHAPTER V

'GOOD MORNING!' cried Ashley Stone as Ella closed the door to the Green Room behind her. Ella's hair was drenched with rain, even though the flat she shared with Greeny was only a hundred metres or so from the café.

'Ashley,' Ella said, 'what are you doing here so early?'

'I wanted to see you.'

Ashley's tone was uncharacteristically cool and calculated. She looked perfectly composed. Ella noticed that Ashley's hair had survived the elements intact and her eyes were so bright you would never have known she had been up until three, dancing the night away with Scott.

'I'll get us some tea,' Ella said, disappearing into the kitchen. Greeny looked over from the stove.

'Good morning, sleepy head!' she laughed. 'Rough night?'

'How long has Ashley Stone been here?' Ella hissed.

'The best part of an hour, I'd say. She was asking me all about Alex before.'

'Where *is* Alex?'

'It's Sunday, remember? He won't be in until this evening.'

Ella decided that she would have to face up to Ashley, whatever it was she wanted. Arming herself with two mugs of tea, she backed out of the kitchen, leaving Greeny to her breakfast orders.

'So, how did you enjoy the party?' Ashley asked Ella as she sat down opposite her.

'Oh, it was great,' Ella said, wishing she could sound more convincing.

'I didn't see you and Teddy together much,' Ashley said.

'Oh?'

'No, in fact, you completely disappeared at one point . . .'

Ella sipped her tea cautiously.

'. . . *after Alex arrived*,' Ashley continued, managing to make the three words sound loaded with meaning.

Ella wasn't in the mood for games. If Ashley wanted a fight, she might as well get it over with.

'What's your point, Ashley?' she said.

'My point?' Ashley gazed up at Ella with her innocent blue eyes. 'I'm just making conversation.'

Ella shook her head. 'I don't think you got yourself out of bed early and sat here for an hour waiting for me just to make conversation.'

'OK.' Ashley set her mug on the table and

took a deep breath. 'I think you should know that we're all very concerned about your relationship with Teddy.'

Ella wanted to smile. Ashley sounded like she was representing the United Nations.

'Of course, he's far too proud to mention it himself, but it hurts him to see you with Alex. It makes him look foolish. It makes all of us look rather foolish, don't you think?'

The words were too carefully rehearsed — scripted no doubt by Ashley's mother. Rowena Stone must have decided that Ashley had the best chance of pulling Ella into line.

'I think you're making a mountain out of a molehill, Ashley.'

'Really? Alex walks in and you abandon Teddy and the rest of us, without so much as a word, to be with him. And then you both disappear and when you finally come back, a whole hour later, you seem unable to hold a reasonable conversation. I think we deserve an explanation!'

'If Teddy and I are having some problems, it's up to us to sort them out,' Ella said.

'Quite,' Ashley nodded. 'I think you know what you have to do, don't you?'

With that, she pushed back her chair and wrapped her sweater around her shoulders. She stood up and walked to the door, fishing an umbrella out of the stand.

'It's time to choose,' Ashley said, reaching for the door handle. 'Teddy or Alex?'

She pushed open the umbrella and disappeared out on to the beach. Ella didn't know whether to laugh or cry. She reached for the mug of tea and took a gulp.

'What was all that about, then?' Greeny said, having deposited two plates of bacon and eggs at another table.

Ella shrugged. 'It seems that I've fallen out of favour with the Stones.'

'What have you done, love? You didn't go to the party wearing mismatched shoes, did you?'

Ella would have smiled but she was too angry, too confused. 'Ashley says I have to choose between Teddy and Alex.'

'Oh.' Greeny pulled out a chair and sat down. 'I didn't think it had come to that so soon.'

'It hasn't. At least, I don't think it has. I mean I think it's over between Teddy and me. But I've scarcely spoken two sentences to Alex since we met.'

'Maybe Ashley Stone has looked into her crystal ball and seen the future!' Greeny laughed. 'Don't take it too seriously, love. Remember, Ashley's younger than you. If you want my opinion, she's been watching too many soap operas. You'll sort this out with Teddy . . . and Alex. In your own time.'

Greeny reached out and squeezed Ella's shoulder. Ella smiled. She felt better, but it was still a rough way to start the day.

*

Greeny sent Ella back to the flat to get a proper rest. The clouds were beginning to clear. Greeny was right, Ella decided. Ashley *was* a queen of melodrama. Perhaps her visit was simply a misguided attempt to support her big brother. Having gained a better perspective on everything, Ella found it easier to rest and soon drifted off into a smooth, untroubled sleep.

She was woken by a hammering beneath her window. She leapt up and looked through the glass. Teddy was standing below. She drew back, her heart racing. Had he seen her? What did he want? Trying to calm down, she walked through the hallway and down the stairs to the door. He had just started to knock again, when she pulled open the door.

'What's the matter?' she asked.

He said nothing, staring at her with wild eyes. At first, she thought he was angry. Then, she realized that it wasn't that. He looked as if he had had a terrible shock.

'You'd better come in,' she said, pulling him lightly across the threshold and closing the door behind him. She led him into the kitchen.

'Greeny sent me,' he stammered. 'I have some bad news.'

'OK, tell me!'

'There's been another attack,' he said, his face quite expressionless. 'This time it was a boy.'

CHAPTER VI

TEDDY REACHED over to pull her towards him, but she resisted.

'Who?' was all she said.

'Chris Kamen,' Teddy said, his expression changing from shock to scorn. 'You know the singer from that local band . . . the Disenfranchised . . .'

'The Disenchanted,' Ella corrected.

'That's right! Hippy twaddle. Have you got anything to drink?' He opened the refrigerator and pulled out a can. He offered one to Ella, but she shook her head.

'Is he going to be all right?' she asked.

'There were complications this time,' said Teddy, flicking up the ring-pull. 'He was out all night in the rain. They're keeping him at the hospital.'

Ella was silent. She felt uncomfortable at him being here. She knew she was going to have to face him sooner or later, but to have him drag her out of bed like this, with this news.

'Great party last night!' Teddy said, apparently unaware of her unease. 'I swear my dad's a genius. Have you ever seen anything like the Cave before?'

'Teddy, we have to talk.'

'We are talking.' He drained the can.

'I mean talk about us,' she said, fiddling with the belt of her dressing-gown.

'My favourite subject!' he said, smiling. Catching the seriousness of her expression, the smile faded and was replaced by a frown. 'What's up, Ella?'

How could she put these feelings into words? She didn't want to hurt him. But she couldn't go on pretending that nothing had changed.

'I think it's over, Teddy.'

'What?' He looked more astonished than anything else.

'I don't want to go out with you any more.' She had to keep it simple, straightforward.

'Is this about these attacks, this "vampire"?'

'No.'

'But everything was perfect, is perfect.'

'No, Teddy,' Ella persisted. Was he really that blind or was he just refusing to accept the truth?

'I've never wanted anything . . . anyone, the way I want you,' he said. Maybe he really thought it was true.

'But I don't want you.' She hadn't meant it to sound so harsh, so final. As the words left her mouth, she could see she had dealt him a fatal blow. He looked devastated.

'I know what this is about,' he said, a nasty edge creeping into his voice. 'It's about Alex, isn't it? You're getting rid of me so you're free for him!'

Ella shook her head. She wasn't about to go into her feelings for Alex with Teddy.

'Well, go right ahead!' he snapped angrily. 'See what a great time you have with Mr Mystery.'

He charged out of the kitchen and raced down the stairs towards the door. Ella followed. What could she say to calm him down?

'Just be careful,' he said as he reached the door. 'You don't know anything about him. For all you know, he could be the vampire.'

With that, he opened the door and slammed it hard behind him. Ella clung to the banisters and collapsed in a heap, fighting back tears. It took her a moment to realize that they were tears of relief.

'That new young doctor from the hospital was in tonight,' Greeny said, carrying a stack of dirty plates into the kitchen. 'Apparently Chris's condition has stabilized.'

'Thank goodness,' Ella sighed.

'What about *your* condition?' Greeny said, checking on a pan of soup. 'How are we going to sort you out, eh?'

Ella took another carrot from the colander and started chopping it.

'You don't have to do that, love,' Greeny said. 'Alex and I are all right, aren't we?'

Alex flipped a couple of burgers over on the grill and nodded. Ella wished that he would say something to comfort her. After all, this was partly his fault. If he hadn't made such a hasty exit from the party . . . If he hadn't come to St Dove's in the first place . . . But it was no use. She couldn't stay angry with him.

'You know what I'd really like?' she said, suddenly brightening. 'A ride on the Harley!'

'Any time!' Alex said, slipping the burger into a bun and spooning barbecue sauce on top.

'How about right now?' Ella said, setting down the knife on the chopping board.

'Done!' Greeny declared. 'It's pretty quiet tonight. I think I can cope on my own.'

'OK,' Alex said, washing his hands. 'We'll drive down the coast. There's somewhere I'd like to show you, Ella.'

Minutes later, they were riding along the coast road. Ella had her arms wrapped tightly around Alex's waist. She had given over all her trust to him. She had no control. They were both wearing helmets so it was difficult to speak to each other, but that suited Ella just fine. She wasn't in the mood for talking. It was the speed she had craved and she wasn't disappointed.

She lost track of how far they travelled. The scenery seemed hardly to change except for the undulations of the cliffs. To start with, she noted the names of the towns as they entered and left them. After a while, she was happy not to know where they were.

Finally, Alex drew the bike to a halt. It was like coming to the end of a brilliant fairground ride. Ella felt a sudden sense of loss as the speed died away.

'Come with me,' Alex said. 'The best views are from up here.'

He didn't wait for her and she had to run to catch him up as he headed across the green to the cliff. As she reached the edge, she gasped. The sun was just about to sink below the horizon and the sea was dark, save for the last golden shards of daylight, floating away.

Ella sat down beside Alex on a rock. He seemed content just to watch the sinking of the sun in silence. She turned her eyes out to sea and let the flickering of the light on the waves carry her away. So, this was what he saw when he looked out to the ocean.

She must have drifted off to sleep. When she came to, she realized that her head was resting on his shoulder. Embarrassed, she pulled away and stood up. Beyond the cliff was only darkness now. She might have been standing at the edge of the world.

'Ready to go back?' he asked, holding out his hand to help guide her through the darkness to where they'd left the bike.

The journey back seemed to take only half as long. Before she knew it, they were retracing their route along the cliff road that led down into St Dove's. If only they hadn't come back so soon. She could have happily driven all through the night.

Suddenly, the bike started to judder. Alex brought the Harley to a standstill. Then he tugged off his helmet.

'Damn! I knew I should have filled up with gas before we came back.'

It was an easy enough mistake to make, but where did it leave them? It wasn't far into town, but the bike was too heavy to push. They couldn't leave it there.

'You go down and get some petrol,' Ella said. 'I'll wait here.'

Alex shook his head. 'I'm not leaving you here.'

'I'll be fine, honestly.'

He gave her a disbelieving look.

'We'll just have to wait here until someone drives past. What time is it?'

'Nearly eleven. Greeny will be tearing her hair out.'

'Someone will come along soon.'

They waited by the side of the road. The moon gave them some light and it was a warm night. All in all, thought Ella, things could have turned out a lot worse.

'Alex?'

'Yes.'

'Why did you come to St Dove's?'

45

Finally, the question she had been burning to ask since she had first seen him.

'I had to get away.'

'From what? And why here?'

He sighed and seemed to be searching for the right words. But before he could speak, they heard the sound of a distant engine. Someone was coming down the road. Alex ran over to attract the driver's attention. The car came into view, a red MG, slowing as it reached Alex. Ella looked across and saw, with a sinking feeling, Ashley and Scott in it. Ashley shot Ella a killer look and whispered something in Scott's ear. They laughed and Scott pushed down hard on the accelerator and drove away.

Alex turned to Ella. She shrugged. It would have been worse to have to accept help from them, she supposed.

'You were saying,' she said, trying to pick up the thread of their conversation, 'why you had to come here.'

'Yes?' Alex looked distracted. Clearly he wanted to keep his attention on the road.

'It's OK if you don't want to tell me,' Ella said.

Alex turned to her, his face bleached white by the moonlight. His eyes burned with a strange intensity.

'My parents died. OK?' And then, before she had the chance to recover from the first shock, 'Actually, they were murdered.'

His eyes bore straight into hers. She was still grappling with the impact of what he had said. She had created some sort of fantasy around him, without thinking that the secret he was carrying could be something so terrible.

'I'm sorry,' Alex said, suddenly agitated. 'I didn't mean to upset you. Look, could you just stay here for a minute or two? I think . . . I just . . . need to be alone.'

He slipped into the shadows and, in an instant, was gone.

Later That Night . . .

SUDDENLY, I KNOW what I need. I'm not sure how much time I have or where I will find it, but there is no alternative.

First, I must get away from here. I move quickly through the darkness. And then, I see it, hidden under the cover of the trees. The red MG. I can't help smiling. It is a perfect solution.

I slow my movements as I approach the car. It is empty. They must be near by. I carry on.

I must focus. Time is short. They are close now, I can feel it. They must be near the cliff-edge. I push on through the trees until I see them. They are together. That was to be expected. I shall have to divide them. Who shall I choose?

I rustle the branches to let them know I'm there.

'What was that?' That's her.

'Where?' Him.

They pull away from each other.

'Wait here!' he tells her.

As he comes towards me, I give him the slip. He disappears into the trees as I emerge from them, ready to surprise her. I'm behind her now and she hasn't even seen me. I reach out and clamp my hand over her mouth.

I clear the hair away from her flesh and move my mouth towards the vein. She puts up a struggle. I am impressed. Then, I manage to restrain her and bury my lips in her neck.

I feel her resistance draining away. She grows limp so that I am holding her up now. I could go on for ever, tonight. But I have to go, to return to the place where I am expected. I can explain a brief disappearance but nothing more.

And so, I leave her. Just in time.

'There's nothing to worry about. There's no one . . .'

I hear his words. I would love to stay and watch his reaction but I must get back. I hear his scream slice through the air. I smile. I can't help myself.

CHAPTER VII

A s the scream finally faded into silence, Ella heard the sound of branches snapping. Alex ran out into the road, panting heavily.

'Alex! Are you OK? Was that you?'

He was unable to speak but he shook his head.

'But look, you're bleeding!'

Still without speaking, he followed her gaze to his shoulder where there was a smear of red. He touched his fingers to the wound at the base of his neck and saw the red on his fingertips.

'It's nothing,' he said, huskily. 'I scraped against a branch.'

Ella began to walk over to him. He turned away. They both froze as they heard the sound. An engine. They looked up the road. A pair of headlights swooped down, almost blinding them. As the shock of the light receded, Ella turned and signalled to the truck to stop. The truck drove up to them and slowed to a standstill. The driver, a boy of Alex's age, leaned out of the window.

'Are you in some kind of trouble?' he inquired.

'My bike broke down,' Alex said. 'Could you give us a lift into St Dove's?'

'Sure!' said the driver. 'I'll give you a hand to load the bike in the back.' As he stepped down from the truck, he held out his hand.

'Mike Morgan.'

Alex and Ella introduced themselves as they climbed up beside Mike on to the bench seat at the front of the truck.

'You play in the Disenchanted, don't you, Mike?' Ella said.

He nodded, starting up the engine.

'You know what happened to Chris?'

'How's he doing?' Alex asked.

'Not too good,' Mike replied.

'I'm sorry,' Ella said.

'I think he'll pull through,' Mike went on, adjusting the rear-view mirror. 'In the mean time, we're supposed to be playing at Weston-bury this weekend. Question is, can we find ourselves a new singer?'

There was silence.

'That sounds awful, doesn't it?' Mike said, his tone of voice changing. 'I mean, he's my best friend and I'm fretting about some gig. It's just . . . we've been working towards this for the past two years. We were finally getting it together . . . and now this. He'd want us to be there. I know he would.'

He shook his head. 'That's why I was up here. I was waiting . . . to catch the vampire.

Crazy, huh? But the vampire has struck three times on this stretch.'

Ella looked over at Alex but he was staring coolly out of the window. She shivered.

'I don't know what I was thinking of. It's a good thing you guys came along. I'd have probably ended up as the next victim −' Mike turned to Alex − 'if I hadn't heard you scream.'

'I didn't scream,' Alex said.

Mike's jaw dropped and a curious expression took over his face.

'Then, who?'

'Mike, slow down! Look!' Ella cried.

Mike stamped his foot on the brake before looking out to see the figure standing in the middle of the road, waving his arms frantically.

'Another breakdown?' Mike said, slowing the truck.

'I don't think so,' Ella said as Scott ran over to the window. His hair was dishevelled and his shirt and jeans were torn and stained with dirt . . . and blood.

'You've got to help!' he yelled. 'Please help me! It's Ashley. She's been attacked.'

Ella thought Scott was going to tear the door off the truck. But when he realized they were going to help, he turned and disappeared into the trees.

Minutes later, he returned, carrying Ashley in his arms. Ella gasped. Ashley lay there, limp as a rag doll, her long blonde curls matted and out of shape. Her arms dangled lifelessly, as pale as china. And there, at the base of her neck, were the tell-tale marks.

'They're going to kill me,' Scott said to Ella. 'You know what they're like.'

In spite of herself, she felt sorry for him. He'd been scared half to death by the attack on Ashley and now he would have to tell her parents what had happened. As Mike drove the truck up the driveway to the Stones' house, Scott began to panic.

'Ella, won't you come in? You could help. You know them.'

She shook her head. 'It would only make things worse. You know how they feel about me right now. I'm the last person they want to see.'

And so Scott carried Ashley out into the darkness alone. The others watched from the truck as he approached the front door. It opened and lights flooded the windows. Ella caught sight of Teddy running out to help Scott. Richard Stone was close behind, followed by Rowena. In the confusion, none of them seemed to notice the truck pull away down the drive.

'I'll take you guys home,' Mike said.

They came to Alex's house first and he and Mike lifted down the Harley. As they did so, Alex said, 'This probably isn't the right time, but I used to sing in a band at home.'

'Great!' said Mike. 'We're rehearsing at my place tomorrow . . . I mean this afternoon. Why don't you come over?'

Ella listened to Mike giving Alex instructions on how to get to his house. At least something good had come out of all the madness.

'Good-night!' Alex called out to her. He seemed brighter than before.

'Good-night!' she called back. 'Thanks for the ride.'

The words died on her lips as the front door opened and an old man appeared. His face was lined and he was frowning. He said something to Alex. Ella couldn't catch the words but he seemed to be angry. Alex snapped back and followed the old man inside. The door slammed shut behind them.

'Gabriel Culler looked pretty angry,' Ella said as they drove away.

Mike nodded. 'He certainly did.'

'I've never really seen him up close before.'

'Haven't you been into his shop?' Mike said and continued as Ella shook her head, 'It used to really spook me when I was a kid. All these clocks all over the place. All set at different times. I remember going in there with my dad once and this cuckoo shot right out at my ear. I had to be carried away, screaming.'

He laughed at the memory. Ella found herself laughing with him, welcoming this release from the tension.

'Of course,' Mike said, 'Culler will be in his element now.'

'What do you mean?' Ella could see the Green Room up ahead and, beyond, the flat. A light was on in her bedroom window.

'Haven't you heard the stories?' Mike said, halting the truck.

'What stories?'

'Well, apparently, old Gabriel Culler is an expert on vampires.'

Ella thanked Mike and wandered up the path to the flat. The events of the evening ran through her head like a videotape on fast forward. Certain moments, certain words came back to her. She remembered what Alex had said about his parents being murdered. She heard the scream cutting through the air. She saw the expression on Alex's face as he glanced at the blood on his fingertips. And she saw again Gabriel Culler's anger as he pulled Alex inside. And, through it all, the same question pounded away inside her head. If Gabriel Culler was an expert on vampires, who or what was Alex?

CHAPTER VIII

THE NEXT MORNING, Ella woke to find that Greeny had already left the flat. She dressed quickly and hurried to the Green Room. She found her in the kitchen, furiously chopping up vegetables for a soup.

'I think you owe me an explanation,' Greeny snapped.

Ella saw that her eyes were bright with tears. Clearly, she was more upset than angry.

'I was so scared,' she said, letting go of the knife. 'I thought . . . I thought . . .' But her mouth refused to make the words.

'I know,' Ella said, going over to hug her. 'I know. I had no right to do that to you. Things just got out of hand.'

She relayed to Greeny the strange events of the previous night, omitting a few details that she thought would only upset her further. Greeny listened attentively. When Ella stopped speaking, Greeny was silent.

'Well?' Ella prompted.

'What can I say? I don't understand any of this. I never believed in vampires. I still don't know what to think. I don't know how we can protect ourselves. All I do know is I'm very scared.'

Ella reached over and hugged Greeny again. They held each other close for a while.

'What's all this then?' Alex said, striding into the café, followed by Mike and the other two members of the Disenchanted.

'Hi, Alex,' Ella said, turning. 'Well, Mike, did he make the grade?'

'He was fantastic,' Mike replied, looking in awe at Alex.

Alex looked embarrassed and busied himself introducing Patrick, the bass player, and Steve, the drummer.

'I need a favour,' Alex said to Greeny. 'Could I have Saturday night off to go to Westonbury?'

'Well, Saturday night is our busiest time, you know. And I'm not sure I approve of all that *loud* music . . . of course you can!' she laughed. 'I wouldn't let you miss this chance for anything, my love.'

Later, when Mike and the other guys from the band drove off home, Alex and Ella went for a stroll along the beach.

'It's good to see you making a life for yourself here in St Dove's,' Ella said.

'It's all thanks to you.'

'What do you mean?' Ella asked, turning and brushing a strand of hair from her eyes.

'Well, if you hadn't wanted to go for a ride last night, we'd never have got stuck on the cliff. And Mike would never have stopped to help us and so I'd never have found out that the band was looking for a singer!'

'I'm not so sure.'

Alex looked at Ella quizzically.

'Don't you believe in fate? That some things are just meant to happen? That however you try, whatever you do, you can't force them and you can't stop them.'

As they walked on, Alex seemed to be considering the proposition.

'I suppose I feel I could have stopped my parents' murder,' he said at last.

He still hadn't told her any more about what had happened and Ella wouldn't push him. Her curiosity about him had changed into something deeper, stronger.

Suddenly, Alex stopped walking. He faced Ella squarely and reached out his arms until they rested on her shoulders. Then, as if in slow motion, he leaned in close and his mouth met hers. He kissed her, gently, on the lips. As he pulled away, she looked up at him in surprise.

'What was that for?'

'For taking some of the guilt away,' Alex said. 'I don't know whether I believe in fate. But I do believe in you.'

This time, she pulled him towards her and they kissed for longer. Alex's eyes closed and Ella closed hers too, letting herself float away on the delicious sensation.

When they drew away again, they joined

hands and walked out towards the ocean, coming to a standstill at the water's edge. Ella could feel Alex grow tense. She saw that his eyes were fixed on the foam that travelled across the sand, ending its journey just in front of their feet.

'I've not been this near water since –' Alex broke off.

Ella watched as another wave came in towards them.

'My parents . . . they died at sea,' he said.

'You were with them?' Ella said, suddenly understanding.

'Yes. I was on the boat. But I escaped. I had to –'

'It's OK, you don't have to tell me.'

'No, I want to! I had to escape because I had to save my brother.'

Ella looked at him in shock. This was the first time he had mentioned a brother. She followed his gaze out into the churning surf, sensing his despair.

'But you couldn't save him, Alex, could you? He's dead too, isn't he?'

Slowly Alex turned away from the water and dropped his head.

'As good as,' he mumbled.

They walked back across the beach, hand in hand. Just when his mood had seemed to be lifting, the thought of his brother had depressed him again. Ella found herself full of more questions. Who was this brother? What had happened to him? If he wasn't dead, where was he now? But she couldn't ask Alex any of this, not yet.

As they were nearing the Green Room, Ella saw the familiar outline of Teddy's VW parked on the cliff. Scott's MG slid into view beside it. Teddy came over and stood at the cliff-edge, staring down at Alex and Ella. Ella could feel Alex start to release her hand, but she gripped him all the more tightly. He looked at her questioningly but, ignoring his gaze, she walked on.

By the time they reached the café, Teddy, Scott and Jeff had climbed down the steps. Ella and Alex turned as Teddy strode over.

'Ashley's condition is stable, thanks for asking,' he said, sarcastically.

'We're forming a search party,' Scott said.

'There's a whole lot of kids meeting down here later,' Jeff added. 'We're going to stake out the cliff-top.'

'The vampire has attacked there four times,' Ella said. 'Aren't you afraid you'll be setting yourselves up for the next victim?'

'Will you join us?' Jeff asked.

Ella looked at Alex and then back at the three others.

'We can't come tonight,' Ella said. 'We have to work here.'

'But afterwards?' Jeff persisted. 'We're going to stay up there all night!'

Ella shook her head. 'No. I'm not coming,' she said, moving towards the door of the café.

'What about you, Alex?' Teddy said.

Ella stopped dead in her tracks, turning to see Teddy stand before Alex, his arms folded tightly across his chest. 'You were there last night. You saw what happened to my sister. Will you come and help us stop it happening again?'

Alex didn't reply. He seemed to be looking through Teddy. Ella wondered if he was thinking again of his family, the family he had lost.

'If you're not with us, then you're against us,' said Teddy.

'You would say that,' Ella snapped, angrily. 'That's the way everything works with you. Everything's black or white. Well, it's not that simple, Teddy. It's not that simple. When are you going to get that into that sunburned skull of yours?'

She reached out her hand to Alex, but it was Teddy who grabbed it, seizing her by the wrist and spinning her back to face him. She could feel his hot breath on her face as he began to speak.

'You've changed, you know. You used to be sweet and kind and —'

'No. No, Teddy. I'm no different to how I always was. Perhaps you're just seeing me for real at last. And perhaps I'm seeing you for what you are too.'

LATER THAT NIGHT . . .

THE MADNESS has begun again. It always does, no matter how far I travel. It is as inescapable as the hunger.

They are up at the top of the cliffs now, torches in hand. They think they are the first, but I have been here before with other crowds. The fear is the same, the panic. When will I learn that this is something to be afraid of? That *I* am something to be afraid of?

Even if I hadn't heard in advance of their plans, they would not have tricked me. I shall not walk along the cliff path tonight. There are other paths, other ways . . .

I look over now as the cliffs melt into the distant sky, the moonlight lapping at their edge. I was happy here. Where will I go next? Where is there left to go?

I see the hospital ahead of me. There's a nurse leaving. As she drives off, I walk into the car-park. A sign up ahead tells me what I need to know.

Hospital corridors are the same the world over. The same lino that makes your shoes click in a certain way, the same smell.

It's ridiculously easy to get to where I need to

go. The door, of course, is locked but a moment later, I am on the other side. I'm surrounded by refrigerators. Which shall I choose? What does it matter. I pull open a door and stare at the row of glass bottles. Maybe I should have done this earlier. Maybe then I could have avoided all the madness.

As I walk back through the darkness, I am overwhelmed with melancholy. I have satisfied that hunger but a different one remains. I look up to the cliffs. The torches are still shining.

I look down to the beach. I glimpse a boy and girl walking hand in hand by the edge of the ocean. It makes me unbearably sad. I look away. When I look back again, they have disappeared.

CHAPTER IX

ELLA SAT BY the window, turning the pages of the newspaper without really taking in any of the information. The world seemed a faraway place. All that mattered was what was happening in St Dove's. She felt her world was marked out by Teddy on one side and Alex on the other. It was an uncomfortable place to be.

Alex had set off early for Westonbury with Mike and the others to get ready for their performance that evening. He'd gone to Mike's to rehearse after his shift in the café the night before. They had said Ella could sit in but she had decided to wait to see them up on the stage. She was both excited and scared for Alex.

Gazing through the window, she saw that the beach was empty. It was rare for there to be no early morning surfers or walkers. Perhaps the rest of St Dove's was exhausted from the night before. Even Greeny was sleeping in. Ella felt like she had the whole town to herself.

Folding up the newspaper, she came to a decision. She grabbed an apple from the bowl on the counter and headed out of the Green Room, locking it behind her.

The air was brisk, if not quite chill and Ella was glad she had brought a sweater. She realized with a shock that it was an old cricket sweater of Teddy's. For a moment, her blood ran cold. Then she decided not to be silly. She could return it to him later.

She walked up the cliff path, not encountering a soul, and took the fork that led into town. The high street was empty too. The shops were shut up, with 'closed' signs hung behind the glass doorways. She came to a stop in front of a shop-window, noticing a light inside.

Ella rang the bell and waited. There was a 'closed' sign here too, but that didn't matter. She knew he was there. She rang the bell again and rapped on the window-pane. Soon she heard footsteps.

The door opened. He didn't look surprised to see her. His lined face scarcely made any expression as he held the door open for her.

'I thought it would be you,' he said, somewhat irritably. 'I knew you'd come, sooner or later.'

Ella stepped inside and he locked the door behind her. Her eyes darted around the room, from one clock-face to another. She could see why Mike had been scared as a child. There was something forbidding about all the old clocks, as if they sat in judgement of her. They seemed to hiss at her as she walked past them.

'Come this way, Miss Ryder,' Gabriel Culler said, leading her into a workshop at the back.

Ella stood before a long desk, littered with bits and pieces of old clocks and watches, tools and rags. Culler lifted an ornate carriage clock off a chair and indicated to her to sit.

'You've been seeing quite a bit of Alex.'

Ella nodded. 'We've become friends.'

'Have you now,' said Culler, picking up a small wristwatch and dropping it into his palm.

'He's told me about his parents, and his brother.'

'Oh.' Culler still refused to be surprised.

'I need to know more,' Ella said. 'You must see that. I want to help him but I have to know more. And I can't ask him. That's why I'm here.'

Culler moved the silver watch around in his palm, weighing her words.

'All right, Miss Ryder,' he said, at last, 'I'll tell you what you want to know. But first, there's something I must ask you.'

He looked up into her eyes. She quivered. He had exactly the same eyes as Alex.

When Ella got back to the Green Room, she saw that Greeny had opened up. Scott and Jeff were sitting, drinking coffee, by the window.

'How did the stake-out go?' she asked them.

Their eyes met hers but neither of them spoke. Frowning, she turned away and saw Greeny, standing in front of the kitchen door. There was a strange expression on her face.

'Come in here,' she said.

Ella followed her into the kitchen. Something important had obviously happened, but what?

As she entered the kitchen she saw Teddy sitting at the table. He was pale and drawn in a black turtleneck. She was used to seeing him in bright T-shirts. He looked older suddenly.

'I think you should sit down,' Greeny said, pulling out a chair for herself.

'Would someone tell me what's going on?' Ella said, leaning against the counter.

Teddy looked sombrely at Greeny. She nodded. Carefully, he pulled down the turtleneck. There, at the base of his neck, were two small holes in his flesh, ringed with dried blood. His neck was red and raw.

'No!' Ella cried. 'No. It's not possible.'

Greeny reached out a hand to steady her, but Ella shook it off.

'I don't believe it!' she said, but the wound seemed real enough. 'All right, I've seen enough. Get out of here.'

Teddy walked out of the kitchen without looking behind him.

Ella found herself crying. 'I don't understand,' she said, burying her head in her hands. 'I just don't understand.'

'It happened on the cliffs,' Greeny said calmly. 'The usual place. Teddy had heard something. He wandered away from the search party, through some bushes into a clearing. He realized his mistake but it was too late. Thankfully, the others quickly saw that he was missing and found him. He was unconscious, but they rushed him home and he made a quick recovery. They decided to call off the search party.'

Ella heard the words but she couldn't let them take hold.

'Last night,' Greeny continued, 'Ashley Stone began talking about what happened to her. The last thing she remembered seeing was Alex, in the bushes.'

'It isn't him. He isn't the vampire!' Ella sobbed.

Greeny wrapped her arms around her.

'It's hard to accept, love, of course it is –'

'No!' Ella pushed her away and ran out of the kitchen.

As she ran out of the café, Teddy darted up from his chair. Ella went on to the beach, towards the sea. She could feel Teddy running behind her, closing the gap. She ran on, losing momentum, until she came to the water's edge. He was level with her now and grabbed her, spinning her round to face him.

'You *have* to believe this,' he said, 'for your own sake if nothing else. How do you know he won't attack you? No one is safe until he leaves St Dove's. No one.'

The wind dried the tears on Ella's face and he held her as her breathing started to slow.

'It all makes sense,' Teddy said. 'It all fits,

like a jigsaw. The attack on Juliet happens just before he shows up. Then, bingo, he gets her job in the café. Then Chris Kamen gets attacked and Alex just happens to be available to take his place in the band —'

'You're forgetting Lucy Vale,' Ella interrupted. 'What was his motive for that?'

'It's the exception that proves the rule,' Teddy said, still holding her tightly. 'You were up on the cliffs the night Ashley was attacked. You know it had to be Alex. And then last night, he attacked me. It's not hard to figure out why, is it?'

Ella didn't answer.

'Because he knew you were going to come back to me. OK, so we needed a break from each other. I can see that now. But you were always going to come back. I knew that. And he did too.'

Ella felt the rush of tears seizing her again. She was so confused by this. If only Alex were there. If only he could speak up for himself.

'It's all right,' Teddy said, drawing her towards him. 'It's all right. It's nearly over. You're safe now . . . as long as you stay away from him.'

Ella pulled away, seeing clearly at last. 'That's why you're doing this! To try to keep me away from him. That's all that matters to you. You'll stop at nothing!'

She turned and marched back across the

beach. She was going to Westonbury. She didn't care what Teddy Stone claimed. She was going to Westonbury. She was going to Alex.

CHAPTER X

As the train pulled into Westonbury station, Ella glanced at her watch. Just after six. The Disenchanted were due on stage in half an hour. There were hoards of people heading towards the concert site and she would have to hurry to make it on time. She tightly clutched the ticket Alex had given her as she jostled through the crowd. It was twenty-five past six once she found a space close to the edge of the stage.

'Watch it!' a girl snapped. 'We've been here since five!'

'Let her stay,' her boy-friend said, smiling at Ella.

Ella smiled back and took her place. Music was blasting from the loudspeakers. Sun blazed down on to the crowd and the friendly boy next to her offered Ella a can of Coke. She accepted it gratefully, enjoying the disapproving looks from the girl. Get a life! Ella felt her mood lift. She felt defiant. She was sick of people telling her what to do, telling her what was safe and what was dangerous. She was perfectly capable of deciding exactly what she wanted.

Six-thirty passed and the Disenchanted did

not appear on the stage. Six-forty and Ella looked around to find more and more people swarming into the arena. The band couldn't have wished for a better crowd. She felt nervous for them and wondered how Alex must be feeling.

Ella thought that the cheers would deafen her as the band finally made their way on to the stage and picked up their instruments. Mike and Patrick strummed a few practice notes on their guitars. Steve sat down behind his drum-kit. Then, Alex came forward to the microphone.

He looked different to Ella. He was wearing the same clothes as usual, a dark shirt and jeans, but his eyes were covered with sun-glasses. Perhaps that's what it was. Whatever, he seemed more confident on the stage. As he cupped his hands around the microphone, the crowd became silent.

'We are . . . the Disenchanted,' he said.

As his words echoed around the arena, the music began and a wave of light shot across the stage. The crowd cheered as Alex began to sing.

He was good. The band was good. Ella found herself swaying along to the music. Looking across the crowd, she saw that everyone was. The atmosphere was electric.

As the last guitar chord brought the first song to an end, the guy beside her turned and shouted over the noise, 'They're brilliant!'

Ella beamed, unable to take her eyes off Alex. He was drinking thirstily from a bottle off water, apparently immune to the crowd's roars of approval.

Two songs later, the Disenchanted's set came to a close. They took a bow, waved to the audience and reluctantly left the stage. But the cheers were so strong that they had to go back on. Delighted, the boys picked up their instruments and launched into another number. This time, Ella saw even Alex smile at the crowd's reaction.

When they finally left the stage, to the disappointed shouts from the audience, Ella made her way back through the crowd to the side of the stage. A security guard stepped in front of her.

'Where are you going?' she inquired.

'I'm a friend of the band,' Ella said.

'How many times have I heard that?' the woman said, looking at her disbelievingly.

'Really, I am,' Ella said.

'Ella! You made it.'

Over the security guard's shoulder, Mike was waving to her. With a sigh, Ella was let through. She ran over to Mike and gave him a hug.

'You were fantastic!' she cried.

'What about Alex, then?'

Mike put his arm around Ella's shoulder and led her through the maze of wires and trucks backstage. Alex, Patrick and Steve were sitting by some steps, talking to . . . no it couldn't be. But it was. As Ella came closer, she heard the American rock god tell Alex what a great future he had. As the star walked off back to his entourage, Mike touched Alex on the shoulder.

'Someone to see you,' he said.

Alex turned and stood, framed by the sunshine. Suddenly, Ella felt nervous. He had become something beyond her reach. She felt embarrassed. He removed his sun-glasses, walked over to her and took her, trembling, into his arms, kissing her. She stopped shaking and kissed him back, running her fingers through his hair.

The band made room for Ella, letting her into their camaraderie. They were thrilled with the crowd's reaction and wanted to hear what she had thought about everything. Together, they replayed the performance over and over again. Ella leaned her head on to Alex's shoulder and curled up, comfortably. She didn't care what anyone said. This was where she wanted to be.

'You can't come in here!'

The security guard was having to ward off more would-be visitors. Her words had become a familiar refrain, but this time there was a note of panic in her voice that made Ella and the others turn.

'No! I said NO.'

'What's going on?' Patrick asked.

Then Ella heard a familiar voice.

'Quick! There he is!'

Teddy and Scott came flying over the barrier as Jeff pushed the guard out of the way. Mike ran to restrain Teddy, but Teddy easily overpowered him, sending him reeling with a punch. Teddy ran on towards Alex. Patrick tried to catch Scott from behind but before he could reach him, Jeff brought him down with a rugby tackle. He fell, catching his ankle in a coil of wires. Steve made a half-hearted attempt to block the others from Alex, but Alex pushed him out of the way, standing defiantly before Teddy, Scott and Jeff.

'Leave my friends alone. It's me you want, isn't it?'

Without speaking, Jeff and Scott grabbed Alex on either side and led him out of the backstage area.

Teddy stood before Ella, calmly folding his arms across his chest. 'I'm doing this for you. I'm saving you from yourself.'

He turned and followed the others, stepping over Patrick as he walked away. As soon as he was out of earshot, Ella turned to Steve.

'We have to follow them,' she said. 'There's no telling what they'll do to him.'

Steve didn't miss a beat, hurrying over to help Patrick out of the tangle. 'We'll take Mike's truck,' he said. 'Don't worry, Ella.'

*

The roof of Teddy's VW was peeled back and it looked for all the world as if four friends were out for a drive.

Mike was having a hard time keeping up in his truck. He, Ella and Patrick were sandwiched on the front seat, with Steve doing his best to sit still in the back of the truck.

'Where are they taking him?' Steve asked.

Ella began to recognize the route. She said nothing but a sign appeared, confirming her suspicions. *Smugglers' Cove. The authentic Cornish experience*.

They followed the VW as it neared the theme park. Teddy drove past the main gates. He must be going in through the back, Ella thought. Sure enough, he drove on around the park's perimeter until he reached a rough, unlit country road.

Ella had never seen this road before but she could make out the various attractions, silhouetted against the night sky. She saw the galleon, poised forever about to sink, jutting out of the fake harbour. And there was the haunted tin mine, perched on the cliff. Where were they going to take Alex?

Mike stopped the truck and, careful not to make a sound, jumped to the ground. The others followed and approached the black VW. They could hear Teddy shouting instructions.

'This way. Quickly!'

As his voice grew fainter, they ran ahead.

They came to a high fence. There was a gate but it was bolted.

'Teddy must have a key,' Mike said, despairingly.

Patrick tried to get a foothold in the fence. He fell backwards and groaned as he hit the ground.

Suddenly, there was an explosion of barking and a dog threw itself at the fence from the other side.

'Who's there? What's going on?' A security guard waved a torch in their faces.

Ella stepped forward.

'I'm Ella Ryder . . . Teddy Stone's girl-friend.' She hated saying the words but it was her only chance. 'He came in through the gate.'

'It's locked,' the guard said, looking at her suspiciously. She hadn't seen him before. Maybe he was new.

'He had a key,' Ella replied.

'Let's get this straight,' the guard said. 'He had a key and let himself in but then he locked it again before you could follow.'

'Something like that,' she said, wishing she had had time to concoct a more likely story.

'I'm not permitted to let anyone into the park after hours, even . . . friends of the Stone family,' the guard sneered. 'You'll have to come back in the morning.'

'No!' Ella said, flinging herself at the fence. 'No!'

Mike reached out and pulled her back. 'It's OK, sir,' he said. 'We understand.'

The guard huffed and called the dog away.

'We can't leave him there,' Ella said. 'They'll kill him.'

'What else *can* we do?' Steve said, dejectedly.

No one spoke. Then, out of the silence came voices, familiar voices.

'That'll keep him out of the way.'

'Now what?'

The key turned in the lock and Ella pushed the others back into the bushes. Teddy stepped through the gate, followed by Scott and Jeff. They walked over to Teddy's car and climbed in. As Teddy started up the engine, Ella heard Scott speak.

'Why don't we just finish him off, now?'

'Just listen to yourself,' snapped Teddy. 'Like some kind of homicidal maniac. I want him out of town just as much as you do, but I'm not going to prison. There has to be another way.'

LATER THAT NIGHT . . .

THE STONE HOUSE is shrouded in darkness. I walk up the driveway, past the VW, and approach the door. It is locked securely but I'm not going to be put off now. In an instant I am standing in the hallway, stepping across the chequered marble tiles.

A long staircase swoops down from above. I begin to climb, pausing on the stairs to look at some of the family photographs that line the walls. Teddy was really quite an ugly child.

I make my way across the landing, then I hear a sound from below. I retrace my steps, noiselessly, and glance down the stairwell. I see Teddy, padding out across the hall, a plate of food in his hand.

As he begins to climb the stairs, I pull back into the shadows. He is coming close now. I hold my breath and let him pass me. He goes a few steps along the corridor and I follow. He stops. I stop. He turns and casually pushes open a door. As I appear inside the room, his mouth falls open.

'What are you doing? How did you . . .' I want to tell him to keep quiet, but he is incapable of saying anything else.

'I wanted to talk to you,' I say, glancing out of the window. I see him eye the doorway, hopefully. I shake my head and move over to block the exit. I'm not about to let him get away. 'What's the matter? Once bitten, twice shy?'

He says nothing. He is shaking all over. I lean forward and inspect the wound. As I thought, it has almost closed.

'You went to some trouble, faking this. It must have been very sore. It's quite convincing – but then you did see the marks on Lucy and Ashley, didn't you?'

'What do you want?' he manages to croak.

'A chance to set the record straight,' I say. 'You see, there was no plan. Not really. It was all pretty random. And I was careful. I never took so much that they wouldn't recover. In a day or so, Juliet and Lucy will start to feel better. They won't remember anything about the attack, and pretty soon life will be back to normal for them. Chris too. Of course, Ashley was found just afterwards so her recovery was quicker. Do you understand what I'm saying? I could have killed them but I chose not to.'

He is incapable of speaking or even nodding. I bend my head towards him.

'You got it wrong, Teddy. You tried to fake it but the joke's on you. Tomorrow morning, when they find you, you'll have real bite-marks to show them . . .'

CHAPTER XI

THERE WAS NO trick lighting or fake mist as Ella made her way down the spiralling stone stairway this time. Her footsteps echoed against the stone. Other than that, the only sound was her own breathing.

As she reached the bottom of the steps, she flashed the torch around the room. There in the corner, she saw him and ran over to him.

They had bound and gagged him and as Ella pulled the cloth from his mouth, she was relieved to see that he was still able to breathe. His eyes flashed up at her gratefully and he began to speak. She placed a finger over his mouth.

'It's OK,' she said. 'Save your energy. You're going to need it.'

She turned him around and worked at the intricate knots that Scott and Jeff had tied. Finally she freed him, pulling the rope away.

'Come on,' she said. 'There's not much time. It'll be light soon.'

He pulled her back, his arms holding her waist. 'Before we go, there's something I have to tell you.'

'All right, but quick . .'

This time, it was his turn to hush her. He

waited until he had her full concentration. 'I'm not the vampire. You have to believe me.'

He looked so solemn that she wanted to laugh. 'I do believe you. I always knew it wasn't you.'

She wanted to turn. There was so much to sort out. They had to get going.

'How? How could you be sure?'

'Because I'm the vampire.'

The words came out casually but their weight was not lost on him. He drew her towards him and held her in his arms. She was stunned. She had resigned herself simply to rescuing him and then leaving town herself. Nothing more.

'How could I have been so blind? Of course. It makes sense, now.'

'Aren't you scared?'

He shook his head. 'How could I ever be scared of you? I love you, Ella.'

He kissed her on the lips, sweetly. She thought she was going to cry. 'What's the matter?'

She didn't answer. Couldn't he see that it was over? He would go his way and she would go hers. It was always like this. Always, she disappeared without trace, like a sand castle swept away by the tides. It had never been so hard before, not since the beginning. She had never met anyone like Alex.

'It's impossible,' she said. 'We can't be together.'

'Why? I have nothing if I don't have you.'

Did he really mean it? She felt herself resisting. It was her only way of protecting herself. If she dared to believe in this dream, how would she ever recover when it crumbled away like all the others?

'You don't understand,' she said, at last.

'What don't I understand? Tell me.'

'There's so much. I don't know where to begin. But it could never work, you as you are and me as . . . what I am.'

He drew away and tore at the back of his shirt, kneeling in front of her, exposing his neck. 'Then make me the same.'

She looked down at the smooth flesh above his shoulder-bone. It would only take a minute or two. All the years of loneliness would be at an end. Her head was spinning with possibilities.

'No, no. I won't do it,' she said. 'There's so much you don't know. I won't do that to . . . to someone I love.'

'But it would be different. We'd have each other . . .'

She turned away. She had made her decision. It was the right decision, the only decision. He would be grateful to her someday.

Gabriel Culler was waiting when they arrived back at the house.

'I've packed your things, Alex,' he said. 'There's money too. It's time you went home. You're ready now.'

The old man smiled and opened his arms. Alex hugged him.

'Thank you . . . Grandfather . . . for everything.' He turned towards Ella. 'You could come, you know.'

'Alex, we've been through this.'

'Let's go through it again. Why can't you come with me? It's as good a place as any.'

'Maine?' Ella thought for a moment. 'America? All right. Why not?'

Alex burst into a smile and took her in his arms, spinning her around the room. She smiled too, even though her heart was breaking. He might believe that they could carry on like this but she knew that their time was limited. Maybe she could go with him now but one day, not far off, they would have to go their separate ways.

'OK, then. That's agreed. Why don't you go down to the flat and pick up some things . . . Oh, what about Greeny?'

It was as if he had run out of steam. Already, he too was seeing the obstacles that stood in their way.

'I'll tell her it's a holiday,' Ella said. 'I don't want her to know the truth.'

'You're sure?'

She nodded.

'All right then. I'll bring the bike down to the Green Room.'

Alex went into his room to pick up the things Culler had packed for him. Culler led Ella along the hallway and reached for the doorknob. As he did so, there was a hammering on the outside.

'Whatever's that?' the old man said, pulling open the door.

Richard Stone marched in. 'Where is he?'

Ella stepped back along the hallway and into Alex's room. 'They've come for you already. You'll have to go ahead without me. Here's what you must do. Remember where we drove to that night on the bike? Drive there and wait for me. I'll pick up my things from the flat and get Mike to take me to you. Now go!'

Alex leapt out through the back door as Richard Stone pushed Culler out of the way and stormed through the hallway. He found Ella in Alex's room and saw the Harley shoot off along the road.

Stone looked Ella in the eye. 'I won't forget this.'

There was no time to say anything more. He ran back out of the house and into his car. Ella followed and saw that Scott and Jeff were right behind him. Other members of the Stones' trusty circle were behind them. What chance did Alex have? She ran out into the street and all the way to Mike's house.

'You've got to help me,' she said. 'I'll explain as we go.'

They jumped into the truck and Mike started up the engine. Ella was about to tell him to drive to the flat when something made her change her mind.

'Follow the cars,' she cried. 'Try to overtake them. Alex *has* to get away.'

Mike rammed his foot down on the accelerator and soon caught up with the car at the back of the pack and overtook it. The cars in front of them were gaining on Alex.

'You'll have to get closer,' Ella said, in desperation. 'They'll be on the cliff road soon, where it's too narrow to overtake.'

She wasn't sure how Mike did it, but he managed to cut ahead of two more cars. Now, there was only Richard Stone's Jaguar and Scott's MG between Alex and them.

Alex surged ahead up the cliff road. Stone followed. Mike tried to overtake Scott's MG but Scott just accelerated.

'Damn!' Mike thumped the wheel.

All they could do now was watch. Ella felt sick to the pit of her stomach. If only Alex could just pull away. She had never wanted anything so much.

But Stone was catching up. They were near the peak of the cliff now. The nose of the Jaguar was almost level with the back of the Harley. Alex turned as the car nudged the back of the bike. As he did so, the bike careered off the road and on to the grass verge. Alex did his best to keep control but the ground was uneven and he was travelling much too fast.

Ella and Mike watched in horror as the Harley hurtled towards the barrier at the edge of the cliff and smashed straight through it. The bike went flying down the cliff, throwing Alex into the sea below and crashing down after him.

'No!' Ella screamed. 'NO!'

One by one the cars drew to a standstill. First the Jaguar, then the MG, then Mike's truck. Stone rushed to the edge of the cliff, followed by Scott and Jeff. Ella jumped down from the truck. Mike tried to stop her but he couldn't.

'I'm so sorry,' Stone cried, his voice now a horrified whisper. 'You have to believe me. I never meant this to happen. It was an accident.'

Ella had nothing to say to him. She turned away and looked down into the sea. There was no trace of the bike or Alex. The waves rolled in on to the beach remorselessly as if it were just another day.

LATER THAT DAY . . .

I STAND AT THE ocean's edge, letting the day die around me. There are surfers in the water, fooling around. The waves are not high enough for surfing. Even I know that. I watch them, sitting on their boards, laughing with each other. Don't they know what happened here before? Doesn't the world mourn with me?

It wasn't meant to turn out like this. I was just trying to teach Teddy Stone a lesson. I knew he was going to be all right. I've never tried to kill anyone in my life. This is like a joke gone wrong. I would do anything to have Alex back. Already I feel so lonely without him.

Greeny wraps her arms around my waist and tries to comfort me. She doesn't understand. How can she?

Realizing that she will get nothing out of me, Greeny turns and wanders back to the café, leaving me alone. I look up and see that the surfers are talking excitedly to each other. One of them is diving underwater. I watch as he calls to his friend and dives again. The other one swims into shore with the boards, throwing them on to the sand. He turns to me.

'We've found a dead body,' he says, returning to the water.

My heart skips a beat. They bring him in, laying him on the sand. His head is cut, just above the ear, but the wound is not deep. He looks, for all the world, as if he is sleeping.

'Did you know him?' one of the surfers asks.

Saying nothing, Greeny leads them away, leaving me alone with Alex.

I crouch down beside him and look at his face. His eyes are closed. The troubled look has gone. He really seems to be having a wonderful sleep.

I remember him as he was this morning, in the Cave. I see him kneeling before me, his neck bared. And I see myself refusing, walking away.

Everything has changed since then. A thought . . . I smile briefly at the absurdity of it, then glance around the beach to make sure I am alone.

Can I do it? Can I *really* do it? Shouldn't I leave him, after all he has been through, to this peace? But how do I know he is at peace? He wanted to be with me. He said so. And I refused because he had other options. Now, what options does he have? But I can give him a way out. Then I won't be alone any more.

I lean over and lift the tangled hair away from his neck. I kneel down beside him, scooping up some water to wash the sand from his flesh.

As my lips brush the base of his neck, I taste the salt water . . .

His eyelids flicker. Soon he is looking up at me and I can see from his eyes that everything is going to be all right. He opens his mouth and seawater gushes out. There's a strand of seaweed caught between his teeth. It makes me want to laugh.

He tries to speak. He coughs and then I hear him try a sound. He breaks off to smile and I smile back. Then the words come.

'I think it's time we got out of this town.'

I don't need telling twice.

FOLLOW ALEX AND ELLA IN THEIR NEW LIFE TOGETHER IN
DANCE WITH THE VAMPIRE

Also in the **DARK ENCHANTMENT** series

House of Thorns
by JUDY DELAGHTY

CHAPTER I

ELAINE PRESSED HER face against the ancient glass of the window to get a better sight of the line of brightly painted caravans. The leaded panes made a diamond pattern on her cheek, and the glass was pleasantly cool in the hot summer afternoon.

'Do you see them, Gwen?' she asked.

Gwen turned from the tapestry she was working and looked at Elaine. 'I can't see anything much from here,' she said.

It was not the way a lady's maid ought to talk to her mistress, and she would have used a different voice if they had not been alone. But Elaine and Gwen had been brought up together, and felt themselves to be more like sisters than mistress and servant. Gwen, at sixteen, was just one year older than Elaine.

'Then come over here, you ape,' said Elaine.

Gwen pushed the needle into the cloth for safety and made her way to the window.

'See?' said Elaine.

'Oh, it's just the gypsies,' said Gwen, disappointed. 'I thought it was something important.'

'Aren't gypsies important enough for you?' asked Elaine. 'Nothing ever happens around here, does it? So we might as well make the most of this.'

'Raggle taggle rubbish,' said Gwen. 'They're all thieves and liars and frauds.'

'*He* doesn't look like raggle taggle rubbish,' said Elaine. She pointed to a young man, walking alongside the lead caravan. He was tall, and upright. His dark hair flowed back and his tread was firm and seemed to carry authority. A flash of silver glinted out from his head.

'Gypsy lovers aren't for the daughter of the Manor,' said Gwen.

Elaine pressed her face against the window again, glad to feel its cold flatness against her cheek.

The line of painted caravans twisted along the road through the parkland that surrounded the Manor House where she lived. It made its way down the slope, across the pasture and towards the river.

'They can't all be liars and thieves,' said Elaine at last.

Gwen paused, considered saying 'No, miss', then relented, and said instead, 'I think so.'

'Let's go and see,' said Elaine.

'What?' asked Gwen.

'I want some excitement,' said Elaine. 'I wish something would happen.'

'Be careful what you wish,' Gwen warned her. 'It might come true.'

'I wish it would,' said Elaine. 'I wish. I wish. I wish.'

Gwen frowned. 'Please,' she said. 'You never know what might happen.'

'No,' Elaine agreed. 'I don't know what will happen, but I'm going to find out.'

'How?' Gwen asked as she returned to the tapestry. 'How will you?' She looked at Elaine.

'From the gypsies,' said Elaine.

Gwen knew what the answer was going to be before she asked her next question, but she couldn't believe it. She wouldn't believe it. She denied it even as she asked. And she denied it loudly when Elaine answered. 'How will they know?' she made herself ask.

'Because I'm going to get them to tell my fortune,' said Elaine.

'No!' Gwen shouted. She surprised herself with the violence of her reaction, but she could not resist herself. Something in her chest seemed to grow tight and painful. 'No!' she repeated. 'You can't!'

'You'll remember who's mistress here, Miss Grey,' said Elaine.

Gwen bit her lip.

The gypsy caravans had arrived at the riverside, and they were drawing into a circle. Children ran around. Men built fires. Women tugged out blankets and rugs, and hung them on the boughs of trees to beat the dust of the road out of them.

Elaine looked out longingly at the busy scene, and wished herself there, in the fresh, warm air. She longed to wade into the water with the children, to tug off her stiff gown and to swim and splash about. Young ladies were not allowed near water. And an heiress was not taught to swim, but Elaine had never allowed that to stop her sneaking off and teaching herself. These days her time was always accounted for and her manners watched too carefully for such activities.

She put her hand to her tightly coiled hair, and she wished she could untie it, let it fall to her shoulders and be free. She looked across to Gwen, hoping to bring her into her dreams, but the needle went swiftly in and out of the fabric, and Gwen's lips were tight and her eyes half-closed in absent concentration.

Elaine's fingers undid her hair, almost without her thinking of what she was doing, or where she was.

Gwen, sneaking a look at her, noticed the lock fall to her shoulders. She sprang up and ran across the room. 'Look,' she said. 'Your hair.'

Elaine gave her a tricky smile. 'Are you going to pull it?' she asked. 'Or did you already, while I wasn't looking?'

Gwen drew herself up. 'You know very well I didn't,' she began.

Elaine hugged her. 'I'm sorry,' she said. 'Friends?'

Gwen softened. She smiled back at Elaine. 'Friends,' she agreed.

'So you'll come with me?' said Elaine. 'That's good.'

'Where?' Gwen was concentrating on a straying strand of Elaine's dark hair.

'To the gypsy camp. To have our fortunes told.'

'No,' said Gwen.

'But something's got to happen. It must. I know it must.' Elaine squeezed Gwen's arm. 'To tell you the truth, Gwen, I can feel it. I know that something's going to happen. I have to go to the gypsy to find out what it is.'

'If we get caught,' said Gwen, 'you'll be in trouble. You'll be watched all the time, kept to your room, forbidden to leave the house.'

'Yes,' agreed Elaine.

'But it will be worse for me. I'll be sent away from the house. I'll have nowhere to go, nothing to live on. Instead of this gown, and a comfortable bed, and meals every day, I'll be homeless and penniless.'

Elaine's face fell.

Gwen's father had died in battle before she was born. Her mother had died as Gwen was born. Gwen had been an orphan before she had finished screaming her way into the world. Elaine's mother had taken her in out of pity. Gwen had no other home, no other family.

'Then I'll go alone,' said Elaine. 'I'm sorry I asked you. It was wrong of me.'

Gwen finished Elaine's hair in silence.

A creak on the landing told them that someone was about to arrive.

. 'Quick,' said Gwen.

Elaine rushed over to the tapestry, grabbed the needle and pretended to sew. Gwen began to tidy the combs and brushes away, as a maid should.

'Come,' said Elaine quietly, in response to the respectful knock.

The door opened.

'Miss Elaine,' said a footman. 'You are called to the Great Hall.' He closed the door.

They looked at each other in wonder.

'What?' asked Elaine.

Gwen spread her hands in helpless silence.

'They only ever use the Great Hall for business,' said Elaine. 'Important business.'

'So why should they want a woman there?' said Gwen, with a bitterness that even surprised herself.

'Come with me,' said Elaine. 'I'm afraid.'

'I'm not summoned,' said Gwen. 'They won't let me in.'

'I need you there. Hide behind the arras.'

It was an old hiding-place. They had often stood together behind the thick brocade curtain. The Great Hall was a place of secrets – adult secrets – men's secrets. So they had made sure, when they were children, that they should find out what those secrets were. Mostly they were boring secrets. Rent collecting from the tenants. Wills signed in front of witnesses and attorneys.

Once, only once, the secret had been exciting. Elaine's father, as Lord of the Manor and Magistrate, had held a court and tried a man for stealing a loaf of bread. The punishment was death, usually. But this time the thief was allowed off with only a beating. Gwen and Elaine still remembered the pitiful gratitude the man had shown, and the tears of joy his wife had shed. But they also remembered the savage flogging he had received, the blood on his back . . . and the screams. They had not gone back to the Great Hall after that.

So Gwen hid behind the arras when Elaine stepped into the Great Hall and saw her father and mother, and the attorney who made out their wills, and the three strangers, with the fair hair and pale skins, who stood by, waiting with them.

'Ah, Elaine,' said her father, and he put out his arms to welcome her. 'This is the most important day of your life . . .'